How Bronwen Got Her Smile Back

By Bronwen Elizabeth Madden
Illustrations by RKS Illustrations

How Bronwen Got Her Smile Back

Dedicated to my Grandmother, Sheila James.

I would like to thank the following people for their support and inspiration: Pam Becker, Catherine Pearson, and Naomi Minahan.

Part One:
A Smile Is Lost

Suddenly, and without warning,
Bronwen **lost her smile.**

Where, oh where, did her smile go?

Was it stolen?

Who would have stolen it?

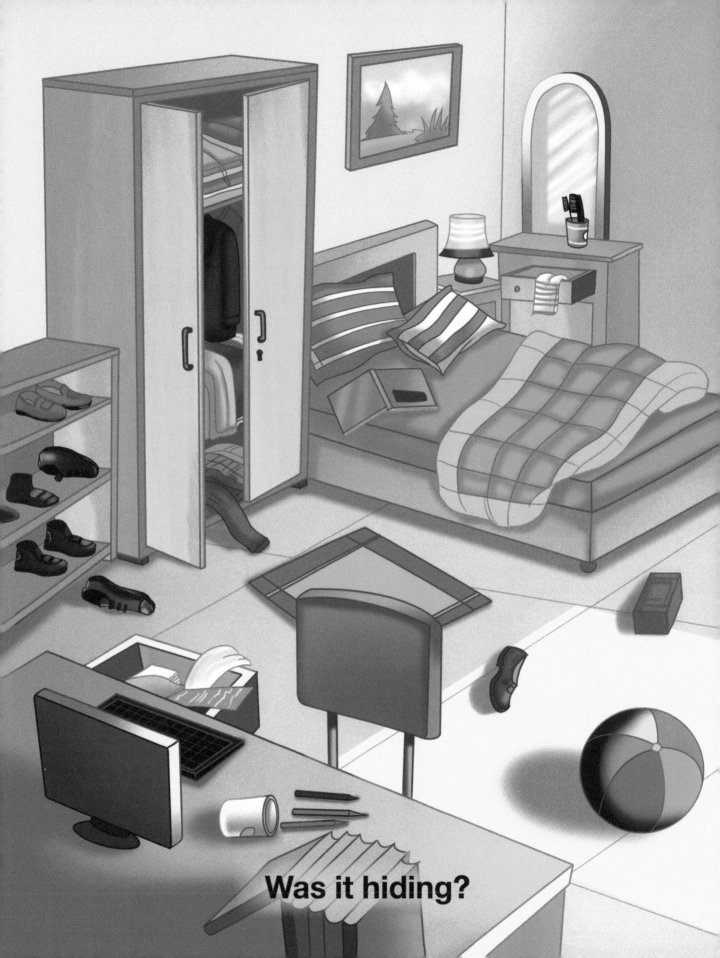

Was it hiding?

Where would it hide?

Did Fluffy eat it?

It must be lost.

Part Two:
Hunting For A Smile

Was it under the bed?

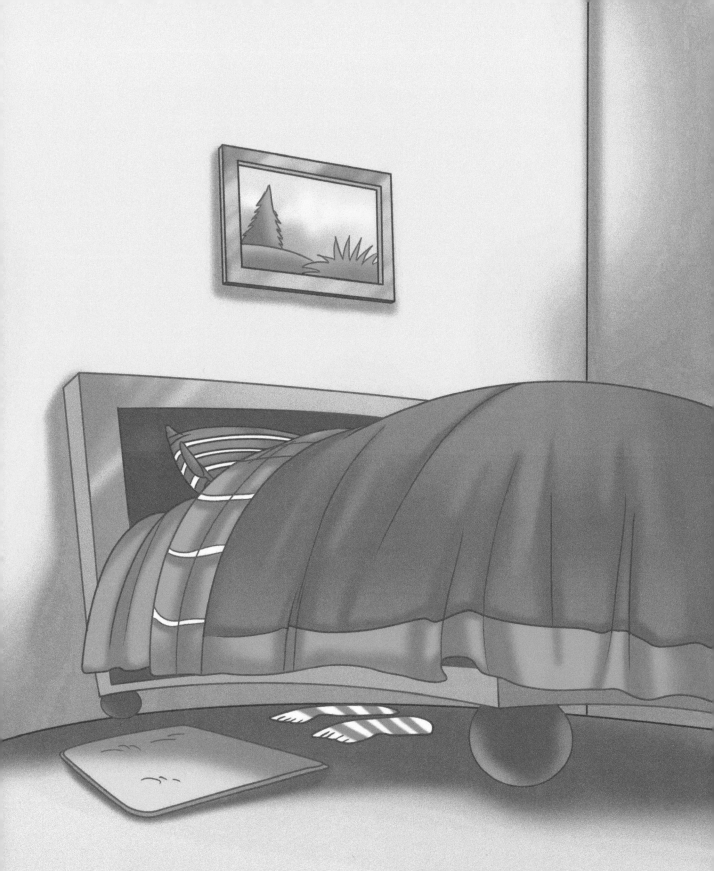

No, but what is under the bed?

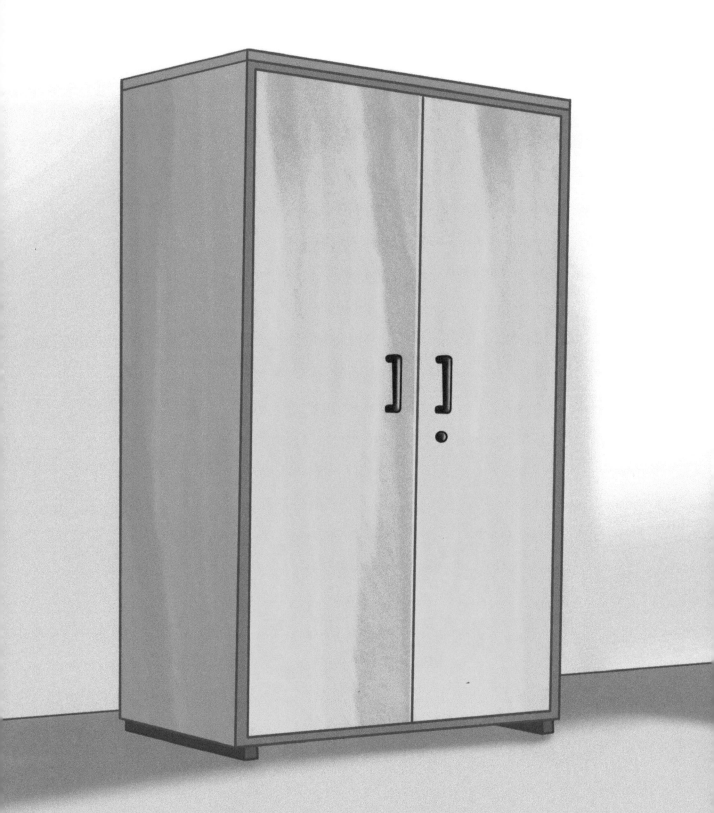

Was it in the closet?

No, but what is in the closet?

Was it under the sofa cushion?

No, but what is under the sofa cushion?

Was it in the laundry hamper?

No, but who is in the laundry hamper?

Part Three:
A Smile Is Found

**Maybe her smile was not
in a particular place?
The doorbell rang and
Bronwen went to answer it.**

Her friend Catherine was
standing at the door.
She had a big smile on her face.

And at that moment,
Bronwen found her smile!

**A smile is a gift of kindness
we give others and ourselves.**

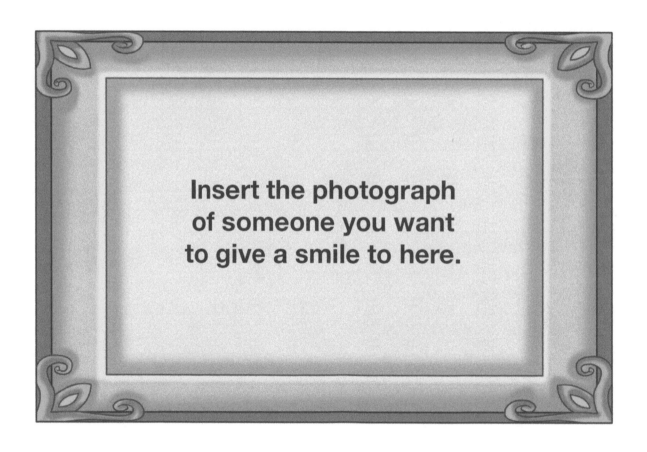

Now, who can you give a smile to?

Bronwen Elizabeth Madden is the author of *How Bronwen Got Her Smile Back*. She is from the rural Missouri Ozarks.

CPSIA information can be obtained
at www.ICGtesting.com
Printed in the USA
BVHW021156090520
578196BV00001B/2